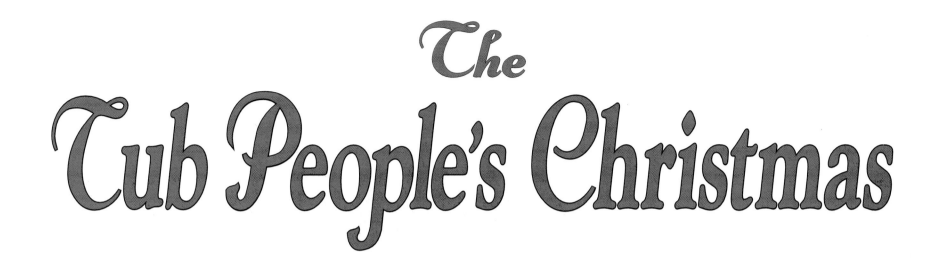

The Tub People's Christmas

by PAM CONRAD

illustrations by RICHARD EGIELSKI

A LAURA GERINGER BOOK
AN IMPRINT OF HARPERCOLLINSPUBLISHERS

The Tub People's Christmas

Text copyright © 1999 by the Estate of Pamela Conrad

Illustrations copyright © 1999 by Richard Egielski

Printed in the U.S.A. All rights reserved.

http://www.harperchildrens.com

Library of Congress Cataloging-in-Publication Data

Conrad, Pam.

  The Tub People's Christmas / by Pam Conrad ; illustrations by
Richard Egielski.

     p.   cm.

  "A Laura Geringer book."

  Summary: The frightened Tub People witness Santa's visit on
Christmas Eve, and even though they do not understand what is happening,
they become beautiful ornaments on the Christmas tree.

  ISBN 0-06-026028-9. — ISBN 0-06-026029-7 (lib. bdg.)

  [1. Christmas—Fiction. 2. Santa Claus—Fiction. 3. Christmas
trees—Fiction. 4. Toys—Fiction.] I. Egielski, Richard, ill. II. Title.

PZ7.C76476Tv 1999   98-53466

[E]—dc21   CIP

                                              AC

1 2 3 4 5 6 7 8 9 10

❖

First Edition

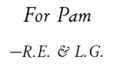

For Pam

—*R.E. & L.G.*

It was a dark winter night. The curtains were closed against the wind and cold, and the Tub People stood on a low wooden table before the fireplace. There were eight of them all in line, the father, the mother, the grandmother, the doctor, the policeman, the grandfather, the child and the dog.

"I am sleepy," said the Tub Child.

"Shhh," said his mother.

"But I want to go to sleep," he said.

The policeman tapped his foot lightly. "You must be quiet! We have to stand guard!"

The Tub Child sighed and closed his sleepy eyes. The wind whistled way up in the chimney.

"But why are we standing guard?" asked the Tub Grandmother. "We need our rest."

"We're standing guard because we are standing guard," answered the policeman.

"Well, I'm not standing guard much longer," said the Tub Mother. "This is quite ridiculous."

The Tub Grandfather leaned close to his grandson and whispered, "Whatever you do, don't go to sleep. Here. Take this." And saying so, the Tub Grandfather pressed a silver hook into the Tub Child's hand. "You might need this tonight."

Before the Tub Child could ask what he meant, the sound of the wind whistling in the chimney changed. There were footsteps and thumpings, and then the sound of someone puffing and straining.

"This is it! This is it!" yelled the policeman.

The fireplace blew out soot and cold air, and then with a crash two black boots landed on the hearth. Before the eyes of the startled Tub People a large man backed out of the fireplace.

"Stand guard! Stand guard!" shouted the policeman. "Who goes there?" But his voice was very very small.

The Tub Grandmother laughed, and the Tub Child hid behind his grandfather.

The large man turned and began to slide the table away from the fireplace. "Hang on there, folks," he said. The Tub People jiggered and trembled and bobbled and tipped, and by the time the man turned back to the fireplace they had all tumbled over on their sides. The Tub Policeman even rolled off the table and landed on the floor.

"Help! Help! Call in the helicopters!" he shouted.

The Tub Child watched as the man reached way up into the chimney. First he pulled down a tremendous sack that landed with a thud.

The Tub Child was frightened, and drew even closer to the Tub Grandfather.

"Don't be afraid, child," his grandfather said. "Watch, now."

Then the Tub People watched as the man reached into the fireplace once more. Again he strained and muttered, but finally, in one great rush of wind and pine, a tree slid from the fireplace and opened like a big umbrella into the room. Its long branches flopped everywhere, and as the big man lifted it, a pine branch swept across the low table and sent all the Tub People flying.

"Help! Help! Stay together!" But they were scattered everywhere. The Tub Child skidded far from his family.

His mother called, "Don't worry, honey. I'm coming."

And his grandmother said, "Just stay where you are."

But the Tub Father called to them, "Oh, no. Look who's here!"

Standing in the doorway, with her nose to the air, was the big dog. She made a soft *woof* sound. This was the same dog that liked to toss them into the air and catch them in her mouth. The Tub Dog barked and barked at her, but his voice was even smaller than the policeman's.

"Why, hello there, pooch," the man said.

The Tub People watched as the man turned back to his work. He began pulling strings of popcorn out of his coat pockets, and golden pinecones out of his vest pockets, and glass balls out of his pants pockets. The big dog sat at his feet watching.

But then, she suddenly saw the Tub Policeman near the chair. In an instant she pounced on him, held him gently between her teeth and tossed him in the air.

"Help! Help! Call headquarters!" the policeman yelled. "Where's my backup?"

The man turned from the tree. "None of that, now," he said softly. He gently took the Tub Policeman from the dog's mouth and dropped him into his empty pocket. Then he noticed the other Tub People scattered about. "Well, well, well," he said, and one by one he picked them all up and dropped them in his pocket—the father, the mother, the grandmother, the doctor, the child, the grandfather, and the little Tub Dog.

It was dark in the pocket, dark and deep, and the Tub People huddled together to wait. They could hear the man humming to himself. They could hear the big dog trotting around the tree. They waited and waited, swaying here and there in the big dark pocket. And then it grew very quiet. And very still.

"What do you think is happening?" the Tub Child asked.

"I'll take a look," answered the Tub Policeman, and climbing up, higher and higher, he reached the edge of the pocket and looked out.

Just then the man reached into his pocket and pulled out the policeman, who left without a sound. He reached in again and pulled out the doctor. The Tub Father was next. "Don't worry," the Tub Father called. "I'll be back." And then the Tub Mother. "Oh! Oh! Oh!" The Tub Grandmother was after her. "Goodness me," she said, and just before the Tub Grandfather was taken, he said to the Tub Child, "Do you have your hook, boy?"

"Yes, Grandfather." And trying to be brave, the Tub Child lifted the Tub Dog in his arms, held tightly to his hook, and waited. Finally the man's hand felt around the pocket once more, and pulled him out.

"Why, you have a hook," the man said. "That's good. I will put you on the top." And at that the man placed the Tub Child at the very top of the tree with his little hook looped around a small branch.

The Tub Child was wide-eyed! Wonder-struck! Below him, spread out like a mountain beneath its snowy peak, was the most glistening, shimmering sight he had ever seen.

Holding the Tub Dog tightly to his side, the Tub Child watched as the man emptied his sack of presents under the tree, patted the dog and stood there admiring his work. Finally, with barely a nod, the man stepped back into the fireplace and disappeared.

"Good-bye," the Tub Mother called.

"Good night," said the policeman.

"Merry Christmas," said the Tub Grandfather.

The wind howled around the chimney and down into the fireplace, sending in a puff of soot. Then it grew very quiet, very still.

The bright and sparkling tree stood proudly in the middle of the room, piled beneath with presents, strung with popcorn, and circled by a small train.

Then very softly, from the top of the tree—

"Momma?"

"Yes, honey?"

"What are we doing?"

And the Tub People laughed.

"We're standing guard!" said the Tub Policeman.

And everyone in the tree laughed—the mother, the popcorn, the father, the candy canes, the grandmother, the star, the grandfather, the camel, the doctor, the policeman, the boat, and at the very top, in a circle of lights, the Tub Child and his dog.